LP. - 9 -27- 07

94
1

95
////

96
7

07
7

ILL40
1

10
7

· HARCOURT BRACE & COMPANY ·

1919–
1994

· SEVENTY-FIVE YEARS ·

PORTRAIT OF

Mary

PORTRAIT OF

Mary

Nikki Grimes

HARCOURT BRACE & COMPANY

New York   San Diego   London

Requests for permission to make copies of any part of the
work should be mailed to:
Permissions Department, Harcourt Brace & Company,
6277 Sea Harbor Drive, Orlando, Florida 32887-6777.

Library of Congress Cataloging-in-Publication Data
Grimes, Nikki.
Portrait of Mary/Nikki Grimes.—1st ed.
p.   cm.
1. Mary, Blessed Virgin, Saint—Fiction.
2. Bible.   N.T.—History of Biblical events—Fiction.
3. Christian women saints—Palestine—Fiction.   I. Title.
PS3557.R489982P67   1993
813'.54—dc20   93-23695

The text was set in Garamond #3.

Printed in the United States of America

Designed by Kaelin Chappell

First edition

A B C D E

For Nancy, Drew, Chris, Becky, and the family of
artists that form Montage.

Behold,
the virgin shall conceive,
and bear a son,
and shall call his name
Immanuel.

ISAIAH 7:14
(KING JAMES VERSION)

*A*rise, shine; for your light has come, and the glory of the Lord has risen upon you. ◨ Violence shall no more be heard in your land, devastation or destruction within your borders; you shall call your walls Salvation, and your gates Praise. ◨ And on that day a great trumpet will be blown, and those who were lost in the land of Assyria and those who were driven out to the land of Egypt will come and worship the Lord on the holy mountain at Jerusalem.

ISAIAH 60:1, 18; 27:13

 THE BLAST OF THE

ram's horn pierced the air, informing all within the pre-cincts of the Holy City that a new moon was soon to appear. The sound agitated the flocks of the shepherds gathered at the sheep market near the city wall. The ner-vous bleating of hundreds of sheep, the measured palaver of shrewd widows wrangling over the price of fine linen in the marketplace—these were the sounds of Jerusalem, heartbeat of the Jewish nation. Here lived the stubborn survivors of generations of oppression and religious perse-cution: slavery in Egypt under the pharaohs; the destruc-tion of Jerusalem by the Babylonians; the sacking of the Holy Temple; and the abomination of the Greek Epipha-nes who desecrated the Temple by shedding the blood of pigs upon the holy altar. Rome was hardly the worst oppressor, only the most recent.

By the first advent of Christ nearly two thousand years ago, the sons of Abraham were weary of being ruled by lascivious and barbaric foreign kings who had no regard for the Jewish religion, and who summarily poisoned, hung, or beheaded their own siblings for political profit. Herod the Great, puppet king of Judea, was no better than the rest. Forever embroiled in political intrigues, Herod had his own wives and sons executed for fear of their rivalry, meanwhile bribing Antony and Cleopatra to look the other way. This man called himself a Jew but was no Jew at all. (His father was Idumaean and his mother Nabatean. Far from being Jews by birth, the Idumaeans had been forced to adopt Judaism by John Hyrcanus, a Jewish priest-king. Herod, then, was a Jew in name only.) A perfidious, godless man by all accounts, he had even dared to build a bridge connecting his palace to the Holy Temple of Jerusalem—this was utter blasphemy!

How long, O Lord? *cried the Jews, longing for the overthrow of Rome and an end to the treachery of men like Herod. Hadn't the Prophet Isaiah spoken of a savior who would come in power and might to rain down justice upon the heads of the nation's enemies, one who would claim the Holy Hill of Zion for the Jewish people once and for all? Where was this promised "Jehovah, Man of War," "the king sent from heaven who would judge every man in blood and splendor of fire," this "King Messiah" described in the Talmud and the Midrash and all the*

Holy Scriptures? These teachings were the bread and meat of every Jew, especially those who clung most stubbornly to the faith of Abraham, Isaac, and Jacob, for it was their faith that had sustained them.

The Jews were right to believe that their God, who had delivered them in the past, would do so again. By the time Rome appointed Herod king of Judea, prayers for the coming of God's Anointed had risen to a crescendo, and those prayers did not go unanswered—though few people living then thought to look for that answer in Nazareth.

Nazareth was little more than an insignificant city, hidden in the mountains above the lush valley of Jezreel. There were no grand palaces, no wealthy precincts here where one might expect to find a descendant of King David's royal line. Rather, this was a city of lowborn peasants, of poor, unlettered Galilean farmers and shepherds.

Yet Nazareth was a place of natural beauty that lent itself to a life of prayer and silent meditation, blessed to have running through it the Via Maris—a road which was part of the major caravan route that ran from Acco to Damascus. Traders in precious gems and gold, perfumes and purple cloth, silk, sandalwood, and spices from such places as Egypt, Arabia, Persia, Phoenicia, Lebanon, and

Syria traveled this route. They brought with them diverse costumes and customs, foreign goods and foreign gods, so that the people of Nazareth had a taste of worlds beyond its borders.

What's more, Nazareth enjoyed some small distinction as a place where priests on their way to the Temple in Jerusalem gathered to prepare themselves with periods of prayer and fasting. Many of Israel's caretakers of Mosaic law and scripture passed through the local synagogues, making their instruction available to any with an ear for the things of God. Here, then, in this plain town of Galilee the ministers and the merchants of the outside world met. Even so, no highborn Pharisee would consider Nazareth a suitable abode for the King of Kings, Lord of Lords, and Savior of the world!

Yet, this very Nazareth was to be the backdrop against which the great mystery of the Virgin Birth unfolded, a mystery that involved a carpenter named Joseph, and Mary, his bride-to-be. Mary, daughter of Anna and Joachim, was destined to become the most revered female figure in the history of the world.

Since many have undertaken to set down an orderly account of the events that have been fulfilled among us, just as they were handed on to us by those who from the beginning were eyewitnesses and servants of the word, I too decided, after investigating everything carefully from the very first, to write an orderly account for you, most excellent Theophilus, so that you may know the truth concerning the things about which you have been instructed. ◨ In the sixth month the angel Gabriel was sent by God to a town in Galilee called Nazareth, to a virgin engaged to a man whose name was Joseph, of the house of David. The virgin's name was Mary.

LUKE 1:1–4, 26–27

THE LATTER RAINS

of the month of Nisan have seeped into the earth, and God has crowned the heavens with a rainbow wreath to celebrate the spring. Wild lily and narcissus blooms spray the hills with color and perfume, though there is little time to smell or gather them. The only growing things I am likely to be gathering for a while are the stalks of flax that must be cut and dried, and later spun into linen thread. The stalks of flax seem endless.

Breathless, I climb up to the roof to snatch a moment's rest and meditation. After milking goats and sieving grain and harvesting and twice hefting heavy waterpots upon my head I feel more like a woman of forty than a girl of fifteen. The middle of the week drags on, and I long for Sabbath sundown. God of Israel, Maker of Days, how joyful I would be if *Shabbath* could begin right now!

I mop my brow and squint up at the sun, grateful for the shade of the palm that overhangs this house. I reach for my basket of wool and start to spin. I work against the stiffness settling into my shoulders from winding the millstone round and round, grinding barley into meal to bake the family's daily bread. Mother said I'll soon be baking loaves for Joseph, and the notion made me smile.

The home he is making for us is nearly done. Father says it won't be long before Joseph and his companions come to my door to find me veiled and in my wedding dress, anxious for the marriage ceremony to begin. The time for betrothal is almost at an end. And so is this day.

I lay my spinning aside and stretch. Then I hurry downstairs to help Mother prepare the evening meal to seal another uneventful day in Nazareth.

And he [Gabriel] came to her and said, "Greetings, favored one! The Lord is with you." But she was much perplexed by his words and pondered what sort of greeting this might be.

LUKE 1:28–29

 A FULL MOON SAILS

on the horizon tonight, sharing the Galilean sky with more stars than I can number. But I can easily count the hours that have passed since I last studied Joseph's face in long, secret glances between mouthfuls of bread and lentil soup during the meal he enjoyed with my family.

I admire this able carpenter whose massive arms have hewed down olive tree and cypress, whose callused hands have sawed and chiseled and planed the finest furniture in Galilee. I like his often stern and serious manner, a token of his maturity and readiness for marriage. I warm to the tenderness in his eyes. Most of all, I love his love of God.

I wish we'd had a chance to talk privately tonight, but my parents were always within hearing. Then, soon after the platter of grapes and figs had been passed around the circle, the evening ended and it was time for Joseph to return to his own home. But no matter. Only a little time remains before Joseph and I are wed as our parents have arranged. Then, as Mother has told me repeatedly, he and I will share a lifetime of private moments.

I yawn and stretch upon my bed. Then, smiling, I close my eyes and dare to dream: with eyes like mine and wearing Joseph's grin, a band of children skips along the borders of my mind. The dream is sweet and I begin to savor it. Then I awake.

A radiance like fire's glow slips into my room. It licks and seems to burn the whitewashed walls and sears them whiter still. Black beetles scurry, searching for dark crevices in which to hide. And I? My heart has stopped. I begin to rise, then, thinking better of it, lie flat on the dirt-packed floor. My family sleeps nearby. Even so, I feel alone.

"Greetings, favored one!" the Radiance says in a gentle tone. "The Lord is with you."

That voice! Slowly I lift my eyes, lids trembling. I gaze upon what seems to be a man. But no earthly person shimmers with such light. This Holy One can only be an angel of the Lord. His pure, good light envelops me. I raise my hand to shield my eyes, but find my palm translucent. And this white heat! Such warmth pours over me, I know beyond all knowing it comes from Him! *Oh, Holy Father. How can this be that You are in the room with me, and yet I do not burn away or wither!*

"Do not be afraid, Mary, for you have found favor with God."

If only I could breathe! If only I could swallow! The angel speaks on. My fear makes my hearing more acute. Then, as I listen, the terror slips away. *Lord, what would you have of me?*

"And now, you will conceive in your womb and bear a son, and you will name him Jesus."

A son. Now. Now? When I am a virgin? The question passes through my mind, but through my lips? I cannot be certain. Nevertheless, the angel answers me, explaining the unexplainable. "The Spirit of God, Himself, will come to you, and you will be enveloped in pure light." And in that moment, God's Son was placed in my own womb. Now I, a Nazarene, will bear a king. And not just any king, but King of All!

Bewildered, I search for one familiar truth, just one. Then, finding one, I hold onto it with all my reason. *God is my Lord, the Lord my God I trust. And, if this be from Him, then I obey.*

Once again, the angel speaks. "And now, your relative Elizabeth in her old age has also conceived a son; and this is the sixth month for her who was said to be barren. For nothing will be impossible with God."

At last, the angel leaves, his light gently fading till I am once again alone in the dark. Suddenly, I realize that my own breathing thunders in my ears. I feel as though I'd run all the way along the Via Maris to the Sea of Galilee and back.

I pace the floor and rub my brow, as though somehow the rubbing could erase the questions troubling me. All things are possible with God, I know. Did He not create the heavens and the earth, and hang the sun and the moon? Did He not create both man and woman? But this? A child conceived, of God, in *me?*

I shake my head and lie back down to rest. The truth will, in time, reveal itself, I know, and I sense that I will never be the same again.

*I*n those days Mary set out and went with haste to a Judean town in the hill country, where she entered the house of Zechariah and greeted Elizabeth. When Elizabeth heard Mary's greeting, the child leaped in her womb.

LUKE 1:39–41

 I'VE KNOWN PRE-
cious little sleep the last few nights, but sleep is
not what I need most. Among the host of questions
that distract and drive me to my feet, one single
idea stubbornly repeats: *I must go to Elizabeth.* Dismissing all other thoughts, I rouse my mother to
say that I must leave for a while, and tell her where
I'll be. She wakes my older sister to go with me.
I'm in no mood for company but do not argue, for
it is not safe to travel alone.

I don my tunic and my cloak, gather a skin of
water mixed with wine, and pack two loaves of
bread for the long journey that lies ahead.

My sister and I step into the predawn cold, my
eyes straining for a hint of first light that might
reveal the shadowy outline of the road that leads to
Judea.

We travel by donkey through Perea, careful to
avoid Samaria, as would any faithful Jew. We want

nothing to do with those Jews of Samaria who sully the faith of our fathers with belief in pagan gods. Yet with the angel's prophecy ringing in my ears, how can I worry about Samaritans now? What shall I say to Elizabeth?

Elizabeth, I have news, urgent news, to share with you. Or, *Elizabeth, I have a tale to tell you. It's quite incredible, really, but—*

I squint into the sun, thankful that its rising has brought me warmth as well as a clear view of the straight path. If only my thoughts were as clear and as straight as that!

Maybe I shouldn't mention my strange visitor at first. Maybe I should begin by asking Elizabeth if she is, indeed, with child. But, what if she isn't? What if I imagined the message and the messenger himself? What if I dreamed them both?

Though I still don't feel ready, I arrive at Elizabeth's door with the sunset.

"Cousin," I call to her. Elizabeth appears with tears of joy trailing down her cheeks. She hugs my sister and sends her into the house, then draws me into her arms for a warm embrace.

"Dearest Mary," she says, holding me close. "It's

been much too long. Zechariah will be happy to know that you have come."

While she speaks, I feel the baby in her protruding belly leap. Smiling, I step away to study this cousin of mine from head to toe. Her face aglow, she proudly rubs her stomach.

"That our Lord should give you a child now, in your old age—what a blessing!" I say. Elizabeth reddens. For several moments, she fixes me with a curious stare.

"I'm blessed, indeed," Elizabeth finally says to me. "But cousin, of every woman born, you are most blessed of all. And blessed is the fruit of your womb, for God this very day reveals to me that you are soon to be the mother of *His Son!*"

An indescribable peace settles over me, this affirmation more restful than many nights of dreamless sleep could ever be. I slip my arm through Elizabeth's and walk to the well with her in silence. We share a cup of water then stroll back to the house, where we ponder the miracle of our twin blessings late into the night.

ow the birth of Jesus the Messiah
took place this way. When his
mother Mary had been engaged
to Joseph, but before they lived
together, she was found to be with child
from the Holy Spirit.

MATTHEW 1:18

 I KNOW THERE ARE

no answers in the gold and purple sunset, and yet I search the sky hoping for the aid of an unseen hand. I lean against an olive tree and pray, "God of my Fathers! Give me the strength, give me the words to say to Joseph!"

Nearby, Joseph smiles at me, and I wonder if he ever will again.

Will this man of God understand what God has done? Will he believe that I, a virgin with child, am a virgin still?

"Joseph," I begin, then shut my eyes and fall against the tree, as though it could support the weight of both my body and my fear. Terror whispers in my ear, *Joseph is going to divorce you. He will think that you have broken the sacred betrothal vows. He will deliver you for judgment as Mosaic law allows. And when he does . . .*

I bite my tongue until it bleeds, but hardly feel the pain. My ears fill with the shouts too easily imagined. *"Sinner!" "Harlot!"* I can envision the hail of jagged rocks, feel them tearing at my skin, payment for a sin of which I'm blameless.

"Mary?" Joseph whispers anxiously. "Are you all right?" His voice brings me safely back to the olive tree. Determined to shorten my agony, I clench my fists and force the secret from my lips.

"Joseph, I'm with child—*of the Holy Spirit.*" There.

I hurry to explain the angel's visitation, the prophecies spoken, the twin blessing of my cousin Elizabeth no longer barren. I tell Joseph all and cringe as the shadow of disbelief falls across his face and betrayal scars his brow. *How?* is the question in his eyes, but he does not ask it.

"This is a private matter," he says at last. "We will deal with it privately."

I am relieved to know that there will be no public divorce, at least. No humiliating end to our legally binding betrothal. I will not be stoned to death. But death is not my only concern.

I gaze out over the valley of Jezreel and think of Hagar wandering alone in the wilderness, faint and frightened, cradling the baby Ishmael in weak and weary arms. Will I become like Hagar?

Joseph and I walk back to town, his eyes studying the ground. His silence is a mallet that pounds, pounds, pounds against my skull, and all I feel is the blinding ache it leaves behind.

At last, I reach my door. Joseph says goodnight and quickly turns to go, not wanting me to know that there are tears in his eyes.

er husband Joseph, being a righteous man and unwilling to expose her to public disgrace, planned to dismiss her quietly. But just when he had resolved to do this, an angel of the Lord appeared to him in a dream...

MATTHEW 1:19–20

I HEAR MY MOTHER
pad across the hard, dirt-packed floor. That's all it
takes to draw me back from sleep. I squeeze my
eyes tightly shut, reluctant to greet this particular
morning.

"Joseph awaits you at the door," I hear my mother say. I dread facing Joseph in the light of day. I
groan and hope that Mother does not hear me.

I rise slowly, thinking of the shame and sadness
that all too soon will press upon my father's house
and heart. Since the bride-price is already paid, my
father, Joachim, will have to pay a portion of it
back. But that is not the half of what drove me to
my knees throughout the night in fits of prayer,
pleading with the Lord who, I know, is there. "If
only you would speak to Joseph, Lord," I prayed.
But Jehovah did not answer me, except to grant a
few precious hours of sleep near morning.

"Mary," my mother calls, wondering what is keeping me.

I take one long, slow, deep breath before going to the door.

When I look Joseph in the eye, he meets my stare. I note the holy light of God's assurance gleaming there, and hope surges through me. I dare not move or speak.

"An angel of the Lord spoke to me in a dream," Joseph begins. " 'Joseph, son of David,' the angel said to me, 'do not be afraid to take Mary as your wife, for the child conceived in her is from the Holy Spirit.' He spoke to me as clearly as I am speaking to you now!" says Joseph excitedly. Then, lowering his voice to a husky whisper, he adds in an awed tone, "We're to name the child Jesus, for he will save his people from their sins."

God be praised! The inner peace I sought floods me with tears, and I am whole again.

So, Joseph and I will be wed as planned. I am grateful that God's hand has molded my world into a shape more familiar, after all!

VI

*I*n those days a decree went out from Emperor Augustus that all the world should be registered. This was the first registration and was taken while Quirinius was governor of Syria. All went to their own towns to be registered. Joseph also went from the town of Nazareth in Galilee in Judea, to the city of David called Bethlehem, because he was descended from the house and family of David. He went to be registered with Mary, to whom he was engaged and who was expecting a child.

LUKE 2:1–5

FOR THREE DAYS, I have searched the yellow-brown, barren hills around me for a hint of green in the sun-baked mud and rock, but there is none. With no visual distraction, I am free to weigh and measure my misgivings about making this rough journey when I am only weeks, or maybe days away from giving birth. How on earth will I manage this ordeal without a midwife? Without my mother?

Another mile or two, and we'll be there, I tell myself for comfort, praying all the while that I do not lose this child. The ass that carries me stumbles and I lurch forward. A worried Joseph hurries to my side. I hide my own concern behind a grin. "I'm fine," I tell him, then ask if we may stop for a moment.

Joseph hands me the wineskin and I take greedy gulps of water to slake my thirst, though I'd prefer a parched throat to the swelling in my ankles and the grinding pain in my lower back. My flesh and bones are under attack, the baby poking, prodding, pressing against my spine, turning and kicking incessantly, seemingly as anxious as I to reach our final destination.

I shiver underneath my woolen cloak. At least the dry, bright break in the weather has lasted longer than one can usually expect, praise God. All the same, I needn't have risked the freezing trek from Galilee to Judea in the middle of the winter rainy season. Joseph could just as easily have gone to Bethlehem alone and registered with the census for us both. But I could not remain in Nazareth without him. I do not care to bear this child without Joseph at my side.

"Be of good cheer," Joseph tells me, though his own feet in travel-worn sandals are painfully bruised and blistered. "We are nearly at Bethlehem's gate."

Will I ever see the gates of Nazareth again? I couldn't bear to live under the scrutiny I have become accustomed to this year: the stares, the whispers, the jeering, jarring laughter at my back, the gossip.

"Tell us, Mary," women pressed me daily at the market, on the streets, at the well near the city's edge. "When will you and Joseph wed? Or has the marriage taken place already? Surely, there's no need to hurry now!"

The child's life and mine would be simpler in a new place, a town or village far away from scandal, but whether we resettle is up to Joseph, and up to God.

The fertile foothills of the Shephelah outside of Bethlehem are lovely, I am told.

God of Abraham and Sarah, who will hold my hand as I go through the first pangs of childbirth? Mother, I need you!

"Mary," says Joseph in a whisper edged with excitement and relief, "we are here!"

Bethlehem, royal city of David, rises from the wilderness. Herod's castle and mighty fortress dominate the view, towering above a maze of white-washed buildings gleaming in the last light of day. Row upon row of fruit trees, bare in winter, hug Bethlehem's borders, boasting of the land's fertility.

Now I understand why this city is called House of Bread.

Joseph smiles at me, and I smile back. Perhaps we will find more than bread and lodging here, more than a few nights' rest. Perhaps we will come to call Bethlehem home.

VII

*I*n that region there were shepherds living in the fields, keeping watch over their flock by night. Then an angel of the Lord stood before them, and the glory of the Lord shone around them, and they were terrified. But the angel said to them, "Do not be afraid; for see—I am bringing you good news and great joy for all the people: to you is born this day in the city of David a Savior, who is the Messiah, the Lord. This will be a sign for you: you will find a child wrapped in bands of cloth and lying in a manger."

LUKE 2:8–12

 A ROCKY GROTTO
smelling of cattle, wet hay, and dried goat's milk
is not where I'd have chosen to bear my child. A
room in the inn would have been warmer, had there
been a room to spare. But the where of my son's
birth hardly seems important now. He is here, alive
and well, with all ten fingers and ten toes, and he
knows that I'm his mother.

Joseph washes the baby with water from a well,
then gently rubs salt into his tender skin to make
it firm. When that is done, Joseph wraps my son
in bands of hand-embroidered cloth, then places the
little one beside me.

"My baby," I whisper, the pain of childbirth forgotten in an instant. I lie staring into that open
face, love beating out a new rhythm inside my
breast. I am overcome.

The eyes are mine, and so are the color and the
curl of his hair. But his mind? Are his thoughts

already, now, winging their way to—God? But maybe not. I've always wondered what babies think and dream.

I touch him. These fingers that have kneaded bread and stirred the midday pot now trace the contours of the face that I am told is the son of God's!

I take him in my arms, this tiny miracle conceived in me. That God chose this lowly daughter of Israel is a blessed mystery. I am a simple woman, after all, of no particular distinction, though now many in Nazareth say that I should bear the badge of shame. But there is no disgrace in being Jehovah's vessel.

I wrestle with the memory of my neighbors' stinging gossip, then I recall the angel Gabriel's words of prophecy. *What do those gossips understand of Jehovah's plans?* I ask myself. Then, staring into the face of God's own son, I wonder, *What do I?*

VIII

Now there was a man in Jerusalem whose name was Simeon; this man was righteous and devout, looking forward to the consolation of Israel, and the Holy Spirit rested on him. It had been revealed to him by the Holy Spirit that he would not see death before he had seen the Lord's Messiah. Guided by the Spirit, Simeon came into the temple; and when the parents brought in the child Jesus, to do for him what was customary under the law, Simeon took him in his arms and praised God ... ◙ There was also a prophet, Anna the daughter of Phanuel, of the tribe of Asher ... At that moment she came, and began to praise God and to speak about the child to all who were looking for the redemption of Jerusalem.

LUKE 2:25–28, 36, 38

THE SOLEMN SONGS
of the Levite priests in Herod's Temple reach the Court of Women, and the throne of heaven besides. My voice joins in the final chorus as the Purification Rite comes to an end, and I rejoice that Jehovah has provided a sacrifice for me. I am once again ritually clean and free to worship in the Temple of the Lord at any time.

I shift my baby from my left arm to my right, then cross the mosaic tile floor and head for Nicanor, the Beautiful Gate, where Joseph waits for me. I approach the marble steps humming, the Psalm of Ascent still lingering in the air. "Lo, children are a heritage from the Lord, and the fruit of the womb is his reward."

We have already dropped five silver shekels in the money box, and Jesus shall soon smell the aroma of the sacrifice for which we have paid, a sacrifice made to redeem him from the Lord. I hug my month-old baby to my breast, whispering, "My son. My firstborn. My heart!"

I start at the sound of my name. "Mary, over here!" My eyes search the throng of men at the top of the stair. *There!* I rush to meet Joseph halfway so that he may speedily take the child before the priest and present him as the holy law requires. Even now, the priest prepares the altar beyond the Beautiful Gate, in the Court of Israel, where women may not enter.

If I am not mistaken, the white-bearded man standing next to Joseph is staring curiously at my child and me. An old priest, perhaps? A teacher from Nazareth? A friend of my father's? I do not know. As Joseph comes near, the stranger follows. Before I can ask who the stranger is, he, with Joseph's consent, takes Jesus in his arms. The comments the stranger makes are most peculiar. He refers to the Messiah. He mentions my son. He then declares that they are one and the same!

If only I could tame the wild fear that surges through my veins! I cannot breathe, or think, or swallow. The stranger's words sound hollow as they echo in the passageway.

"Master, now you are dismissing your servant in peace, according to your word; for my eyes have seen your salvation, which you have prepared in the presence of all peoples, a light for revelation to the Gentiles and for glory to your people Israel. This child," says he, "is destined for the falling and the rising of many in Israel, and to be a sign that will be opposed so that the inner thoughts of many will be revealed—and, be very clear, young mother, a sword shall pierce your soul before the prophecy is come to pass."

"Joseph," I whisper, once the man has gone. "Who *is* he?"

"Simeon," Joseph answers in a hush. "A devout man of the Lord."

No one can afford to ignore the words of one known to be a righteous man. Even so, I reel from his foretelling. I have no time to think on it before the prophet Anna approaches. I have noticed this widow at the Passover festival many times, so small and frail, with pale skin and secrets tucked in the wrinkles of her brow. "Blessed be Jehovah!" says she. "This holy child shall be the redemption of Jerusalem."

She, too, foresees a future beyond my comprehension.

Dazed, I hold my tongue. I see my perplexity mirrored in Joseph's eyes. I coax him to take the child before the priest as planned while I remain behind in the Court of Women.

My son. My son, I silently repeat, the prophet's words turning in my head. How can I make sense of it? My son, wrapped as any other newborn child in swaddling clothes, will save the nation. Will reveal—*what?*—to the Gentiles, a people who know nothing of our God. My firstborn, who this very moment is being redeemed with the sacrifice of turtledoves, will by himself redeem Jerusalem?

I surrender to the mystery and leave it to the Lord. In the meanwhile, I take solace in a psalm. One verse calms my spirit more than any other. "The secret of the Lord is with those who fear him, and he will show them his covenant."

When? I wonder. *When, oh Lord, will you show me?*

*I*n the time of King Herod, after Jesus was born in Bethlehem of Judea, wise men from the East came to Jerusalem, asking, "Where is the child who has been born king of the Jews? For we observed his star at its rising, and have come to pay him homage." ▣ Then Herod secretly called for the wise men and learned from them the exact time when the star had appeared. Then he sent them to Bethlehem, saying, "Go and search diligently for the child; and when you have found him, bring me word so that I may also go and pay him homage." When they had heard the king, they set out ...

MATTHEW 2 : 1 – 2 , 7 – 9

THE SOFT RIPPLE OF children's laughter beyond my front door reaches me here in my courtyard. A private courtyard is a pleasant place to be after time spent living in a stable. And, though many months have passed since we moved here, I do not take this house for granted.

I rest on the bench Joseph made especially for me, enjoying the midmorning hush. There will be time enough to rush later in the day. For now, I relax with Jesus on my lap. He is satisfied with nursing for a while. I tickle him until he smiles, then bury my face in his curls. "My sweet boy," I whisper. I give him a loving squeeze, then bounce him on my knees and stare at the clay oven nearby.

What should I make for the evening meal? I wonder. *A vegetable stew again? A lentil soup, perhaps, with giant slices of cucumber, leeks, and lots of garlic, just the way Joseph likes it. And maybe fig cakes for dessert.*

Alert as ever, Jesus turns his head at the sound of voices approaching. I look up as Joseph sweeps into the courtyard with a gathering of townsfolk close behind.

"Joseph, what's going on?" I ask.

"Mary, you won't believe this. These Chaldeans, astrologer priests from Persia, or Assyria, or somewhere in the East, have come to see the child."

"What?" I ask. Joseph, out of breath, tries to explain, but before he can say more, they are here. Men of dark complexion, finely dressed in silk and purple tunics, the hems of their garments intricately stitched with threads of pure gold. One of the men is old, one fairly young, I think, the others of an indeterminate age. Each has the look of a sage about him.

"Good sirs," I greet them shyly, worried that they'll think me immodest, as my head is uncovered. Instead, they bow. Then, to my astonishment, they kneel in the dust. Words of adoration are on their lips, an effervescence of praise directed towards—my son?

They call him king and lay royal gifts at his feet.

47

A silk pouch heavy with nuggets of gold, delicate alabaster jars filled with oil of myrrh, more measures of frankincense than I have ever seen poured out in the Temple. *Lord, Jehovah, what am I to make of this?*

Frozen in place, I feel my spirit leave my flesh. I step outside my skin, join the curious townsfolk standing back, looking in. They are as amazed as I by this display. I cannot fathom half of what I see. Did this child come from me?

*A*nd having been warned in a dream not to return to Herod, they [the wise men] left for their own country by another road. ⊠ Now after they had left, an angel of the Lord appeared to Joseph in a dream...

MATTHEW 2:12–13

JEALOUSLY, I GLARE
at Joseph, who lies in restful sleep while I toss and
turn in frustration. *Why does this night feel so full of
trouble?* I carefully review the day, digging about
for the root of my vexation. I grin, remembering
how Jesus, who is only beginning to walk, mim-
icked me this morning when I touched the mezuzah
parchment on the doorpost. I kissed my fingers that
had touched the holy words "The Lord Most High,"
and I laughingly applauded when my little one
brought his fingers to his lips and did the same.
"The Lord shall preserve thy going out and thy
coming in," I recited, and Jesus nodded as if he
understood. Perhaps he did. God only knows. The
child grows so quickly!

Then in my imagination I see Jesus falling, falling as he did today in the courtyard when he
tripped over a toy Joseph had carved for him. The
boy was barely bruised, but when he fell to the

ground, I found myself sweeping him up into my arms and crushing him to my breast protectively, my grasp so tight he whimpered. What frightened me enough to frighten him? I wish I knew. I do my best to quell my disquiet till I am finally able to drift off to sleep.

"Mary!" Joseph calls. I keep my eyes shut until I sense the urgency in Joseph's voice. "Mary, get up!" he says insistently. "The Lord has spoken to me in a dream. We must leave this place tonight. We must flee to Egypt, for Herod seeks the child so that he may kill him."

Suddenly I understand what earlier seemed an unreasonable fear. My son is in danger! Praise God for his clear revelation!

"Hurry!" says Joseph as he helps me to my feet. Together we roll up the bedding and gather up his tools, a few dishes, and our clothing, bundling them haphazardly in the middle of the floor. We are poor people and it grieves me that this hurried flight in the middle of the night means leaving nearly all we own behind.

What if Joseph is mistaken in the vision? We are finally settled here. Bethlehem is our home, now.

It is here that Joseph and I were wedded, here that my son was born. We are just beginning to do well. Joseph's carpentry skills are in greater demand here every day. There are small children nearby my son can play with. And I, always slow to make friends, have found other young women to talk to. And what of my kinswoman Elizabeth, closer to my house and heart than she has ever been—I may never see her again. Leave Bethlehem, *now?*

Nevertheless, my sense of dread remains, and I will not risk the safety of my son. But Lord, flee to *Egypt,* land of our forefathers' captivity? Surely Egypt is no place for a Jew.

"Joseph, are you sure?"

"The vision was clear," Joseph says with conviction.

I bite my lip and turn away to dress the child. When he is ready, I set him on a chair, then feel around the floor for my sandals. My fingers fly, deftly tying the leather laces of my sandal. I would rather undo the knots forming in my belly. Miriam, how you must have felt following your brother to the Red Sea with Pharaoh's army in hot pursuit. Your choice was more difficult than mine: to remain behind and die at Pharoah's hand, or to drown in the sea. But the God of miracles did part the waters, making a way where there was none. He was faithful to our people then. Surely He will save my family now from Herod's tyranny.

I circle the room, memorizing the walls and windows of the first home my husband and I were blessed to share. I stare at the stools and table made by Joseph's hand and say a silent goodbye to this good place. I hold Jesus in my arms and whisper in his ear, "The Lord shall preserve thee from evil, he shall preserve thy soul."

Joseph opens the door and steps into the night. I follow, pausing long enough to kiss the holy mezuzah parchment.

*W*hen Herod saw that he had been tricked by the wise men, he was infuriated, and he sent and killed all the children in and around Bethlehem who were two years old and under, according to the time that he had learned from the wise men. ▨ Then was fulfilled what had been spoken through the prophet Jeremiah: "A voice was heard in Ramah, wailing and loud lamentation, Rachel weeping for her children; she refused to be consoled, because they are no more."

MATTHEW 2:16–18

I FILL MY WATER JUG,
then balance it upon my head. I leave the well and
as I do, two Egyptian women pass me on the road.

"What a tragedy," says one. "Twenty babies
slaughtered! They say that Herod has a stone where
his heart should be!"

My legs wobble under me. I cannot catch my
breath. A tremor rocks my body head to toe, and
before I know what's happening, the waterpot
topples to the ground, shattering in a thousand,
thousand pieces. Trembling, I fall to my knees, digging in the dirt for each clay shard. It is hard to
find them all, especially since I can scarcely see
through all these tears. The jagged edge of a shard
slices my palm and blood spurts from the wound.

Oh God, oh God, oh God. The pain in my soul is
more than I can bear. Why was so much blood shed,
Lord? Why? Why did all those innocents have to

die? And all because of me, Lord. Because I was not willing to sacrifice my son.

I wipe the tears away and rise, surprised by the concern on the faces of the Egyptian women, who watch me from a distance. Composed now, I brush the dust from my tunic and return to the tent to weep privately till I am spent.

My young son, more precious now than ever, hugs me round my knees. *"Ammah,"* he says. "Please don't cry."

At last, my sobbing ceases. I smooth the tousled hair of my child, my life, my joy, and thank Jehovah God for sparing my sweet boy.

Why are joy and grief commingled? I ask myself. There are not enough tears in all the world to bring those babies back, nor words powerful enough to comfort their mothers. Yet the Ruler of Heaven will give Herod his due on Judgment Day, and the Lord himself will bring those mothers solace, for he will wipe away their tears. As for me, I pledge before God to give my all to this child that he might be the kind of son any one of those dear mothers would be proud to call their own.

XII

When Herod died, an angel of the Lord suddenly appeared in a dream to Joseph in Egypt and said, "Get up, take the child and his mother, and go to the land of Israel, for those who were seeking the child's life are dead." Then Joseph got up, took the child and his mother, and went to the land of Israel. But when he heard that Archelaus was ruling over Judea in place of his father Herod, he was afraid to go there. And after being warned in a dream, he went away to the district of Galilee.

MATTHEW 2:19–22

I CLIMB UP YET AN-
other Galilean hill by force of will, exhausted by
this latest journey. With Jesus heavy at my hip, I
gradually catch up to Joseph. My joints complain
with every step, but neither Joseph nor I care
to spend one more minute upon the ass's back.
The beast provides a ride that is, at best, uncom-
fortable.

We pause at the top of the hill, gasping for
breath and drinking in the familiar view. The ter-
raced gardens of the slopes beyond, the avenue of
feathery palms, the neatly ordered orange groves,
the grape vineyards, the fig and pomegranate trees
—my God! I'd forgotten how lovely the hills of
Galilee could be. I wave at the shepherds grazing
in the pastureland below. My eyes pick out the Via
Maris road, on which foreign traders from as far
away as Lebanon and Persia often cross the paths of

priests on their way to Jerusalem. Priests like my kinsman, Zechariah. "Look, son," I say, pointing to the town of my birth. "That's Nazareth."

I didn't think I'd ever see Nazareth again. I didn't think I'd want to. *How restful Nazareth appears.* I need rest so badly. The trip to Bethlehem, the escape from Israel to Egypt, and the journey back again, the constant moving, moving, moving has whittled away whatever strength I thought I had. We had to leave Bethlehem, I know. And we dare not go back to that district of Judea, not with Archelaus in control, he more murderous than his father, Herod. Even Herod did not slaughter three thousand in the Temple of the Lord! We had no choice but to travel on to Galilee. But now I pray that we can settle down for good. If Joseph says that we must move again because he has heard it in a dream, God forgive me, I think I'll scream!

With one final burst of energy, we complete our journey. Suddenly, we are at my parents' door. I see the knot in that old wooden door and grin. That knot is like an old friend. Joseph offered to remove it once, said that he could plane and sand it down until the wood was smooth and fine, but Father refused. "I've grown rather used to that knot," my father said, and so had I.

I raise my hand to knock at the door, but hesitate. I'm no longer the child I was when I left Nazareth an eternity ago. *Mother, will you know me?* I wonder. Do I look any different now? I sent word about the baby's birth long ago. But so much else has happened since I saw my parents last—the peculiar prophecies, the visit of the astrologer-priests, the desperate departure from Bethlehem. What will I tell my parents? Where will I begin?

Mother opens the door and I fall into her arms. She hugs me, bathing me with her tears, her wordless fears for me suddenly washed away. She wipes her eyes and reaches forward tentatively. I tenderly pry Jesus' fingers from the folds of my skirt and nudge him forward.

"Jesus," I tell my son, "say hello to your grandmother."

Just then my father appears, warmly embracing Joseph and me.

"I see you've brought my child back, Joseph, and

with a child of her own! Though clearly Mary is my little girl no longer."

No, Father, I think to myself. *I will never be your little girl again. But I will always be your loving daughter, and your daughter has, at last, come home.*

ow every year his parents went to Jerusalem for the festival of the Passover. And when he was twelve years old, they went up as usual for the festival. When the festival was ended and they started to return, the boy Jesus stayed behind in Jerusalem, but his parents did not know it. Assuming that he was in the group of travelers, they went a day's journey. Then they started to look for him among their relatives and friends. When they did not find him, they returned to Jerusalem to search for him.

LUKE 2:41–45

 DAWN HAS BARELY
broken, but I am already on my way through the
center of the Holy City, anxiously pressing past the
greedy dove sellers who, as ever, line the streets
during Passover. I do not need to purchase doves to
sacrifice today. Joseph and I made our offering for
sin early in the week, though I would gladly make
a hundred more to see my eldest son again. Four
days have passed since we last saw him! We weren't
aware that he was missing until three days ago.
Perhaps we should not have traveled in such a large com-
pany, I think to myself. *It's a wonder we noticed his*
absence when we did.

My eyelids feel heavy after the sleepless night I
spent. Though the hours burned like years, Joseph
wisely said that we should wait till morning to continue our search, and now, once again, we look for
Jesus in earnest.

I dare not consider the thousands of bodies that

separate me from the Temple mount. The sweaty throng flattens me against the city wall. Joseph now far behind, I strain on tiptoes, aching to see the son we have lost, have mistakenly left behind in Jerusalem. *Jesus, how will I ever find you in this multitude? Lord, please lead me to my son!*

I squeeze past jutting elbows, duck deftly between the stalls of the money changers. I'd lift my skirts and run if there were room.

I push towards the Temple. We've looked in all the places a child would be. Besides, there aren't that many children out today, it seems. Where can he be?

There! I see him sitting in a gathering of priests and teachers. When I am nearer, I hear him asking questions about the Torah, questions that many grown men do not know enough to ask.

"Jesus!" I cry, trembling. "What are you doing here? I've been wild with fear. Didn't you even care that we would worry?"

"Why were you searching for me?" he asks in reply. "Did you not know that I must be in my Father's house?"

I look upon this child, this man who'll become

a bar mitzvah all too soon. He answers in a different tone than I expect. He truly thought that I would know where he would be. His father's light gleams in his eye, and suddenly I remember who his father is.

Joseph catches up to me, but I do not turn to him or speak. I keep my eyes on Jesus. I can only stare, my motherly concern lodged in my throat. I silently send up a prayer for strength to bear the mystery of this young life.

Then he went down with them and came to Nazareth, and was obedient to them. His mother treasured all these things in her heart. ⊠ And Jesus increased in wisdom and in years, and in divine and human favor.

LUKE 2:51–52

THE SCORCHING SI-
rocco winds may not reach us here in Nazareth, but the dry heat of August presses on us just the same. I reach for water to quench my thirst. The children playing out front don't seem to suffer from the heat, but Joseph and Jesus must surely be thirsty after a full morning spent in Joseph's workshop. *I will take drinking water to them,* I decide, and head for the courtyard workshop with a full jug and two clay cups.

I find Joseph sharpening an awl on his green slate hone. Jesus works alone with a bow drill, carefully boring holes into the frame of a chair. Later today he will thread woven cord through the holes and across the top to form a smooth webbing for the seat. The chair will meet the highest standards when it is done, for my son has learned the value of fine craftsmanship from Joseph.

I watch Jesus silently. The boy who once bounced upon my knee runs and romps in memory, but the Jesus who works the bow drill is nearly a man. He wears his sixteen years like twenty-one. He's already begun to spend long hours roaming the green pastures, praying and meditating like an old priest or sage. No one else his age is half so serious. His solitary and often solemn nature worries me, though Jesus is as kind and obedient a son as a mother could hope for.

"Mary, why do you stand at the door?" asks Joseph, startling me.

"I thought you might be thirsty. Here." I pour the water out and give one cup to my husband and the other to my strapping son. I smile at the small boy in Jesus' eyes and am delighted when that boy smiles back.

When will even the boy in his eyes disappear? I wonder. *I must enjoy him while he's here.*

*I*n those days, Jesus came from Nazareth of Galilee and was baptized by John in the Jordan. And a voice came from heaven, "You are my Son, the Beloved; with you I am well pleased." ▨ And the Spirit immediately drove him out into the wilderness. He was in the wilderness forty days, tempted by Satan; and he was with the wild beasts; and the angels waited on him. ▨ Now after John was arrested, Jesus came to Galilee, proclaiming the good news of God . . . ▨ As Jesus passed along the Sea of Galilee, he saw Simon and his brother Andrew casting a net into the sea—for they were fishermen. And Jesus said to them, "Follow me and I will make you fish for people." And immediately they left their nets and followed him.

MARK 1:9, 11–14, 16–18

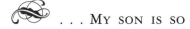 . . . MY SON IS SO

thin . . . so thin . . . forty days without food. He wades into the river and falls into his cousin's arms. Lord Jehovah! He's thinner than a reed. Hold him, John. Hold him. Don't let him go. John! But it's too late. Jesus slips through John's arms and disappears into the depths of the river Jordan. Jesus! I wring my hands and call his name over and over again. A voice from heaven answers saying, "This is my Beloved Son. He is coming home to me." I shake my fist at heaven and scream, No! No!

"No!" I cry out, bolting from my bed. My eyes fly open, I hold my head and sink back onto the bedcovers. Once my heartbeat and my breathing slow, I know that I have just awakened from a nightmare.

I undo my braid with nervous fingers and retwine the gray and auburn strands till I am calm again. This is the third night in a row that has found me shaken from a dream. Sometimes I wish my children did not report to me so faithfully on the strange comings and goings and doings of my eldest son. They say that he hears voices from heaven, that he wars with Satan, that he goes alone into the mountains, and sleeps in the wilderness—no wonder my sleep is troubled by frightful visions of my firstborn.

His disappearing into the hills alone is no surprise. From childhood Jesus has enjoyed the rustling of tall grass and wildflowers in the meadow and the silent splendor of eagles soaring overhead as much as the company of men and women. He's been wandering off alone from the age of twelve. But forty days! He was never gone so long—and without eating! He worries me. It doesn't matter that he's a full-grown man of thirty years. He's still my boy.

I haven't heard the sounds of the saw, the adz, or the bow drill in the workshop for many weeks. Jesus hardly works there anymore, or helps in the harvest. While others gather in the flax and barley crops, Jesus spends all his time fasting and praying and gathering men to be his disciples. I fear that all those years of his training under Joseph now go to waste.

Since I learned of my son's baptism by John, I have been uneasy in spirit. I cannot guess what this foreboding means, but I do not like the feel of it—especially since John was arrested. Will Jesus speak out against Herod as John did and find himself in prison, too? And what of his disciples? Those who once followed after John, now follow after Jesus. But where will my son lead them? Do they know? Does he?

The squeak of my straw mattress sends a lizard scurrying as I rise. I drape a warm woolen cloak about myself, step out into the crisp, cool night, and climb to the roof to pray awhile. I stay to watch the sun rise over Galilee.

XVI

*O*n the third day there was a wedding in Cana of Galilee, and the mother of Jesus was there. Jesus and his disciples had also been invited to the wedding....

JOHN 2:1–2

 LAUGHTER FILLS
this room, a celebration of my nephew's happiness. To attend the wedding of my sister's son is a special joy.

The setting of this blessed event could not be more festive nor the feast more lavish. I join Jesus, his disciples, and other wedding guests at a table spread with bread and cheese, cucumbers and leeks, dates, pomegranates, and melons, salted fish, and a fatted calf, freshly killed and roasted for this most special meal.

I peel a pomegranate and study the bride and the groom. The bride's headband of coins catches the light, but their gleam is dull compared to the light of love in her eyes. I watch the groom remove the garland of flowers from around his neck and tenderly place it around hers. I sigh and cannot help but wish that a young woman as lovely as she were wedded to my son, my eldest son, my firstborn.

The groom's companion stands to offer a song to the young couple. "I come to my garden, my sister, my bride," he sings in the words of Solomon. "I gather my myrrh with my spice, I eat my honeycomb with my honey, I drink my wine with my milk. Eat, friends, drink, and be drunk with love."

"To love!" we cheer and lift our goblets high, as the father of the bride calls for more wine. But the wine, it seems, is finished, though the feasting will continue well into the night. Jesus sits nearby, enchanting the guests with proverbs and tales. As always, his disciples hang upon his every word. I rise and go to him, and whisper in his ear. "It appears that our host has run out of wine."

"Why do you involve me?" he asks, for I have brought to him a feminine concern—the managing of food and drink, and that for the guests of another! I am about to apologize when he adds, "My time has not yet come."

His words, like teeth, sink into my heart. *His time has not yet come? His time for what?* I wonder.

Jesus notes the wounded look in my eyes and immediately regrets his sharp tone. He motions to the servants and swiftly orders six clay jars filled with water to the brim. Puzzled, I stare at him, but to the servants I say, "Do whatever he tells you." Then I walk away, leaving him to his own affairs. He is a grown man, after all.

A few moments later, a goblet of the drink is drawn and taken to the chief steward. *What can be the point of this, plain water in a goblet meant for wine?* I ask myself.

"Ahh!" says the steward, deeply refreshed it seems, though I cannot fathom why. "Everyone serves the good wine first, and then the inferior wine after the guests have become drunk. But you have kept the good wine until now. This," says he, "is the most extraordinary wine in all of Israel."

In awe, I remember how, through a miracle of God, Elijah blessed the widow of Zarephath so that the flour she used for bread and the oil she required for her lamp never quite ran out. This divine provision, I recall, lasted through a long and terrible drought. And now this son of mine has turned water into wine. Surely, this is no less a miracle than Elijah's!

God of Abraham, *Eloi,* can it be that, like Elijah, my firstborn is a prophet, too? *Yes! A prophet and more!* comes the answer from within.

XVII

They went to Capernaum; and when the sabbath came, he entered the synagogue and taught. They were astounded at his teaching, for he taught them as one having authority, and not as the scribes.

MARK 1:21–22

WE MOVED TO CA-
pernaum three days ago, my sons and I. This city
above the Sea of Galilee is where my eldest and his
followers make their home. It is well for me to be
here now that Joseph and my beloved parents rest
with Father Abraham. There is no reason for me to
remain in Nazareth. Besides, if the people of Nazareth will have nothing to do with my son's good
teaching, then I will have nothing to do with them.

Why do they show my son disdain? All he has
done is to declare that the kingdom of God is at
hand. Who would fault a man of God for that? I
am *pleased* that my son professes his love of God and
proclaims his Holy Word, though the manner of it
worries me. Such devotion is, after all, his heritage.
Both Joseph and I are of the royal lineage of King
David, a man who loved the Lord from first to last.

It is *Shabbath,* and I sit in the gallery of the synagogue with the other women who praise the God

of the Sabbath. Below, my son, by invitation, stands, the leather scroll of Isaiah in his hand. He reads, "Therefore, behold, I will proceed to do a marvelous work among this people, even a marvelous work and a wonder . . ."

The congregation says, "Amen," and Jesus begins to teach. His preaching is soon interrupted by a wild man bursting from the crowd of worshipers.

"What have you to do with us, Jesus of Nazareth?" shouts the man. The hairs on my arm stand up. I am suddenly cold, sensing the presence of evil.

"Have you come to destroy us?" the spirit demands in the voice of the man. His clothes are torn and filthy. His eyes are wild and he snarls when he speaks. "I know who you are, the Holy One of God."

"Silence!" says my son, with such command that I am stunned. The force, the power of that one word spoken by him pushes me against the wall. I have all I can do to breathe. *Did this man, this evil spirit, not call my son "The Holy One of God"?*

Before my eyes, the man convulses, foaming at the mouth, then collapses to the floor in a heap. I keep my eyes on him until he rises. He is suddenly soft-spoken, his movements almost languid. He has a peaceful look upon his face and even the trace of a smile. And all at my eldest son's command. *My son!* The other women in the gallery turn to me, as if I could explain this. As if I were not equally amazed.

Dazed, I leave the synagogue with trembling knees. Two of Jesus' brothers, James and Jude, stick close to me. They see that I am very much afraid.

XVIII

*T*hen he went home; and the crowd came together again, so that they could not even eat. When his family heard it, they went out to restrain him, for people were saying, "He has gone out of his mind."

MARK 3:19–21

 DARKNESS FAST AP-
proaches as I near this house that overlooks the
Galilee. My sons close to me, I weave through the
multitude that surrounds the simple dwelling. Inside, my eldest son is telling his disciples God
knows what puzzling parable or strange riddle
about barren fig trees, lost coins, lost sheep, or his
being the Good Shepherd. The words of the prophet
Simeon come to me now—"This child is destined
for the falling and the rising of many . . ."—but
his prophecies remain a mystery. Of one thing only
am I sure: my firstborn makes no sense to me anymore. I worry for him, though. The scribes and
Pharisees clearly resent his popularity. There are
even whispers of a plot to kill him.

I shiver in the chill wind and pull my cloak
tightly round my shoulders. I clench my teeth, determined to hide my fear that somewhere nearby,
the enemies of my son wait in the shadows.

I can see the front door from my place in the crowd, but no matter how loudly I call Jesus' name, he does not notice me. I trouble a stranger to pass the word along until Jesus knows that his family is present. We have come to take him home—for his own good.

Why should he risk his own health by continually healing the blind, the lepers, and the lame and teaching till all hours of the night, meeting others' needs while he himself goes hungry? I'm not persuaded that he's crazy as most Galileans say, but I do know that he can't go on this way.

I look at the worried faces of my other children and realize how somber a circle we comprise. James, Joseph, Simon, and Jude are embarrassed by their brother—I can see it in their eyes. They do not understand him. I, too, am confused as to why he, whom I have raised to be a devout Jew, whom God himself both conceived and blessed, should choose to dine with sinners, tax gatherers, and women of ill repute. The thought of him eating from a loaf of bread touched by a harlot leaves me mute. I wonder time and time again: where did I go wrong?

At last a way is made for me through the crowd.

Just as I reach the door, I hear a disciple say, "Jesus, your mother and brothers and sisters are outside, asking for you." Jesus replies, "Who are my mother and my brothers? Whoever does the will of God is my brother and sister and mother."

What did he say?

I hear his words plainly, but am convinced that a stranger has stolen his voice. *Who is my mother?* Did I not give birth to this child in Bethlehem? Did this Jesus not come from my own flesh?

ow the chief priests and the whole council were looking for testimony against Jesus to put him to death; but they found none. For many gave false testimony against him, and their testimony did not agree. Some began to spit on him, to blindfold him, and to strike him, saying to him, "Prophesy!" The guards also took him over and beat him. As soon as it was morning, the chief priests held a consultation with the elders and scribes and the whole council. They bound Jesus, led him away, and handed him over to Pilate.

MARK 14:55–56, 65; 15:1

THE PASSOVER FES-
tival seems larger this year. Perhaps it is my fevered
imagination that makes it seem so.

Since dawn, I have been in a state of apprehen-
sion. Last night word reached me that my eldest
son had been arrested. He may well have spent the
evening in a Roman jail. I tell myself that his arrest
is a formality, a mistake—he is certain to be re-
leased in a day or two. But if the truth be known,
what I tell myself is not what I believe. My cousin
Elizabeth's son, John, was arrested, then later was
beheaded at Salome's request. His death was not
that long ago. The same end could await my son.

In the narrow streets of Jerusalem is a cacophony:
foreign merchants hoarsely shouting out the value
of their wares, sheep bleating, the heavy footfalls of
Roman soldiers. Over it all, the voices of an angry
mob. Soon I see a host of priests and Temple guards
roughly elbowing past shoppers near the market

stalls. They escort a prisoner. A man, I think. I stand on tiptoes to see if the prisoner might be Jesus, but from where I stand, I cannot see his face.

In a moment, I am caught in the crush of the crowd and carried through the doors of the Praetorium. At last, the people come to a standstill in Pilate's judgment hall. Pilate enters, and the angry voices soften to a milder din. In that relative quiet I summon the courage to ask, "What is going on?"

"The Temple guards have arrested one Jesus of Nazareth," says a boy nearby. "They say he is a blasphemer and demand that Pilate punish him for his crime."

The face of this boy reminds me of my son when he was twelve, when Joseph and I found him in the Temple, speaking with the elders. *It was Passover then, too. Joseph and I searched for you for many days, remember, my son? I almost lost you then. Have I lost you now?*

A clear voice echoes through the judgment hall.

"I find no fault with this man," Pilate declares. "I will have him flogged and release him to you. Is that what you want me to do?"

"No!" voices shout out all around me. "Crucify him! Crucify him!"

No!

"Crucify him!"

"Stop!" I scream, but no one hears me. *My son's blood is what they demand.* I cannot stand to listen anymore. I close my eyes and cover my ears.

The slaughtered innocents in Bethlehem all those years ago—will my innocent son soon join them? I cringe. *Jehovah, You once saved my son from Herod. Please save him now.*

I wait. I listen for a word from God, but there is silence. And with that silence comes the certainty that no amount of prayer will move the Lord to spare my firstborn. Nevertheless, I pray.

So they took Jesus; and carrying the cross by himself, he went out to what is called The Place of the Skull, which in Hebrew is called Golgatha. There they crucified him, and with him two others, one on either side, with Jesus between them. ◼ When Jesus saw his mother and the disciple whom he loved standing beside her, he said to his mother, "Woman, here is your son." Then he said to the disciple, "Here is your mother." And from that hour the disciple took her into his own home.

JOHN 19:16–18, 26–27

AN UNEARTHLY

darkness sweeps across the midday sky over Jerusalem and I welcome it. Today has no right to feel like any other day. I force myself to walk beyond the city gates and stare, despair all but blinding me. All I see is the road that lies before me, and the wretched scene that awaits me at the end.

Three crosses, in silhouette, loom above me as we come near. *How is it that my innocent son hangs among criminals and thieves?* Thank God, I am not alone. My cousin walks to the right of me, beloved John leads the company, and to my left is Mary of Magdala. I yearn for the comfort of my husband—dead these many years. Now it appears that soon I must mourn for another loved one.

How I long to hear him call me Mother one last time!

I wonder if word has reached the other children?

The road has ended and I have all but ceased to breathe. I cannot help but squeeze those hands that firmly hold my own, grateful that they have chosen to share my pain.

My son, my firstborn, is hardly known to me. His lovely beard has been plucked out, blood and sweat form rivulets on his face, and I cannot, for all my searching, find a place upon his body that has not been bruised! But I refuse to scream.

I hear him groan and cannot help but feel the ache in my own belly. My hand flies to the spot where once I felt him kick, a small life lodged in my very womb.

My belly now is flat and wrinkled with age, but no passage of time can ever mar the memory. Nor will I forget that that mouth, now swollen and cracked, once nursed upon my breast. Those arms, outstretched to embrace the world, did once with great joy and abandon wrap themselves round my neck and squeeze—as only a child can, sparing nothing of affection, of love. Trusting that the love would be returned—and it was!

How Joseph doted on that boy! The son who

would follow in his footsteps. Why, he would be the best carpenter in all Jerusalem, if Joseph had his way.

Oh, Joseph! That you were here beside me now!

My eyelids heavy, I sob inwardly. I caress Jesus' feet and lay my head against his legs. John tenderly pulls me away, and as I sway against him, I hear my child say, "Woman, here is your son." And to John, "Here is your mother!" And no other words are spoken between us.

A long-forgotten prophecy comes to me: ". . . a sword shall pierce your soul . . ."

My eyes lock onto my eldest son's one last time until gently, the beloved John leads me away from Golgotha. I do not feel the earth beneath my feet on the somber journey home.

*E*arly on the first day of the week, while it was still dark, Mary Magdalene came to the tomb and saw that the stone had been removed from the tomb. So she ran and went to Simon Peter and the other disciple, the one whom Jesus loved, and said to them, "They have taken the Lord out of the tomb, and we do not know where they have laid him." Then Peter and the other disciple set out and went toward the tomb.

JOHN 20:1–3

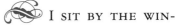 I SIT BY THE WIN-
dow rocking, rocking, rocking, trying to clear my
head. *My son is dead. My son is dead.* I say it to myself
over and over again. Why don't I believe it?

Everything happened so quickly. The judgment,
the crucifixion, the burial—it's all a jumble in my
mind. There was hardly time to weep, or to prepare
his body properly, or to compose a proper lamentation. He was supposed to be alive to march behind *my* funeral bier and cry "Alas! Alas!" How
could he go first?

If only I could stop imagining my son bound in
funeral linens, lying alone in that damp, dark, icy
tomb of rough rock. It could be worse. My son
could lie, as other poor men do, in a shallow grave
where jackals might prey on him. At least no wild
beast or scavenger can disturb his body sealed in a
tomb. I have that to be grateful for, thanks to the
kindness of Joseph of Arimathea.

My son's woolen sash lays across my lap. How odd that John had borrowed it from Jesus the night of the arrest. I stroke it now, fingering the smooth threads, recalling the long hours I spent weaving the delicate pattern. I wish I could do it all again, could make him a new cloak, or a tunic, or a hundred woolen sashes. But my son has no need of clothing anymore.

I hear a voice, or think I do. *Is anyone there? Jesus, is that you?* I call, but it is only John standing in the doorway. His lips move. He speaks very slowly, but his words make no sense to me. "What did you say?" I ask.

"The stone has been rolled away. The tomb is empty. Jesus is not there!"

I'm sure John is mistaken and tell him so. "No," he says. "I was at the tomb. I saw the empty place with my own eyes."

I quietly rise and study John's face for an explanation. Who would take my poor boy's body? Who would steal him in the night?

But there are no answers on John's face.

"There were Roman sentries at the tomb, weren't there? Go," I tell John. "Find Andrew, or Thomas.

Perhaps they know where my son has been laid."

John nods and leaves me sitting by the window tying the woolen sash into fisherman's knots, rocking back and forth, unable to clear my head.

My son is dead. I don't know where they've taken him. What does this mean, Lord? What does this mean?

*W*hen it was evening on that day, the first day of the week, and the doors of the house where the disciples had met were locked for fear of the Jews, Jesus came and stood among them and said, "Peace be with you." After he said this, he showed them his hands and his side. Then the disciples rejoiced when they saw the Lord.

JOHN 20:19–20

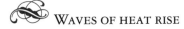 WAVES OF HEAT RISE
from the cooking fire in John's courtyard, the only
part of his household that feels familiar to me. I
shape three loaves of bread, load them on a cooking
sheet, and place them on the fire. I've been sorting
grain, making flour, kneading dough, and baking
ceaselessly since the Sabbath, but the work does not
tire me.

I hardly feel the stiffness settling into my shoulders from winding the millstone round and round,
grinding barley to bake the next loaf of bread. The
familiar routine gives me a sense of comfort.

The neighbors think that I have lost my senses,
because I do not mourn my son by withdrawing
from daily labor. "Why doesn't she give up work-
ing the millstone if she grieves so?" they ask. *They
mean well,* I tell myself. *But few of them have ever lost
a child—and none in so brutal a manner. How could*

they understand? I'm doing the best I can to get from one moment to the next.

My hands covered with flour, I pause, wondering what the hour is. Or the day. I wish my pain were as easily forgotten as the passage of time. But the ache stabs at my heart again, and again, and again. For hours on end I weep for the loss of my son.

Reminiscences, like dear friends, come calling. I think of Simeon and Anna, of the Chaldean astrologer-priests, of the flight to Egypt. *Where did it all begin?* I ask myself, tracing back through the years, before Egypt and Bethlehem, before the death of Herod, back to the days in Nazareth when Joseph and I first prepared to marry. Memory carries me to the night of the angel Gabriel's visitation. After thirty-three years, I can still recite his strange tidings and his promises of a kingdom that would never end.

Is this not an ending?

I remove the bread from the fire, place it on a table to cool. I'm scarcely able to find room, I have baked so many other loaves already. Perhaps John will eat a loaf or two when he comes home tonight.

I hope he is ready to give up this fable, this story about seeing my son. Doesn't he know how much it hurts me? Doesn't he understand that this vision of his is wishful thinking? No one wishes more than I that Jesus were alive. But if he were, surely he would appear to me. *Wouldn't you, my son?*

I collapse into a chair and close my eyes. I open them again and see a man sitting across from me with nail-pierced hands. The rhythm in my breast is a familiar one.

I remember a prophecy of King David. *"You will not abandon me to the grave, nor will you let your Holy One see decay. You have made known to me the path of life."* Is not my son the Holy One of whom he spoke? Did not God's own angel tell me so? And yet somehow I did not fully know until this self-same moment that Jesus is the Messiah, himself the resurrection and the life!

All at once, I know that it's my son I see! A holy light surrounds him. I do not comprehend the miracle, but this is clear: the God for whom nothing is impossible has transformed my firstborn from child of my flesh to the Christ—my risen Lord and King.

Trembling, I fall to my face in fear. I hear the voice of him whom I first taught to speak. "Do not be afraid, Mary," Jesus says. "Your sins are forgiven." Then I feel his warm hand upon my shoulder. I rise and look into his face. There is precious little trace of me left in those eyes. He is no longer mine now, but God's. Yet there is a boundless love and peace washing over me.

Thank you, Lord, I whisper, lifting my hands in praise. *You have done all things according to your word!*

While he was saying this,
a woman in the crowd
raised her voice and said to him,
"Blessed is the womb that bore you
and the breasts that nursed you!"
But he said, "Blessed rather are
those who hear the word
of God and obey it!"

LUKE 11:27–28

NOTES AND ACKNOWLEDGMENTS

Portrait of Mary is a work of historical fiction, based on the Gospel accounts of the life of Jesus Christ as viewed through the eyes of his mother, Mary. To flesh out the bare-bones story of the Holy Family found in the New Testament, I drew from a variety of historical sources, biblical and extrabiblical (see Bibliography for details). I have also woven scripture into the main body of the work as dialogue where that seemed appropriate within the context of illuminating a particular New Testament passage. In a few cases, I have elected to use translations other than the NSRV. In each instance, the translation I chose seemed to offer a clearer understanding of the passage in question.

The names of Mary's parents, drawn from an Apocryphal gospel rather than the Bible itself, are nonetheless widely accepted by Bible expositors. Jude, an abbreviation of Judas, was the brother of Jesus, and author of the epistle of the same name. I here refer to him as Jude to avoid confusion with Judas Iscariot.

To attribute the source of each scripture used as dialogue, whether the use is verbatim, partial, or paraphrased, would seriously detract from the spirit of this work. Instead, I have chosen to acknowledge those sources by including them in the Bibliography.

I should note that the details and time frames in my account contrast sharply with several popularly held assumptions. For example, scripture indicates that the Magi brought three gifts, or types of gift, to the newborn king—namely, gold, frankincense, and myrrh. Thus, it is commonly believed that the Magi were three in number. However, scripture is nonspecific on this point, thereby leaving the actual number open to interpretation. Scholars suggest there may have been as many as eleven wise men. Taking my cue from scripture, I chose to leave the number indeterminate. Again, the decorative Nativity Scenes brought out at Christmas lead many to assume that the Magi visited the Holy Family in the stable shortly after Jesus' birth. Yet a close study of scripture reveals that the Magi actually reached Bethlehem long after the family had left the stable and moved into a house, possibly as much as eighteen months later.

Lastly, I should clarify that the closing chapter is drawn only from my heart and imagination. There is nothing, to my knowledge, in scripture or in subsequent Biblical scholarship claiming that Mary saw the risen Christ. Yet, as a mother who has lost a child, and who understands that unique bond, I am convinced that some such visit took place. I cannot imagine that Jesus would have visited his friends one final time, to bless and encourage them and ease the pain of loss, and not have done as much for his beloved mother. The reader must reach his or her own conclusion.

I gratefully acknowledge the assistance of Charles (Chuck) Olson and of James J. Stewart, Executive Pastor and Life Stages Pastor, respectively, of Rolling Hills Covenant Church, California. Both Dallas Theological Seminary alumni lent their expertise in reviewing the final manuscript for theological and historical integrity. Pastor Stewart's expertise in Bible exposition was particularly helpful.

Special thanks to Joe Yakovetic, who challenged me to complete this work; to Randy Au, Ann Braybrooks, Sandy Brown, Nancy Gary, Doug McIntosh, and Tracy Roeder for their insightful comments and suggestions; to editor Alane Salierno Mason, who deftly guided me through the final revision; to agent Susan Cohen for her faith and enthusiasm.

Heartfelt gratitude to Harcourt Brace President Rubin Pfeffer for catching the vision and running with it.

BIBLIOGRAPHY

Most quotations from the Bible are taken from the New Revised Standard Version, Thomas Nelson Publishers, Nashville, 1990, drawn from the 1989 edition NRSV of the National Council of the Churches of Christ in the United States of America. Notable exceptions are as follows: *Chapter 16*: John 2:3–4, drawn from *Serendipity Bible for Groups, New International Version*. Littleton, CO: Serendipity House, 1988. *Chapter 17*: Isaiah 29:14, Scofield, C. I., ed. *The New Scofield Reference Bible, Authorized King James Version*. New York: Oxford University Press, 1967. *Chapter 22*: Psalm 16:10, Walvoord, J. F., and R. B. Zuck. *The Bible Knowledge Commentary: An Exposition of the Scriptures*. Wheaton, IL: Victor Books, 1983. NIV.

Alexander, Pat. ed., *Eerdmans' Family Encyclopedia of the Bible*. Grand Rapids: Eerdmans, 1973; Carmel, NY: Guideposts, 1978.

Bright, John. *A History of Israel*. 2nd ed. Philadelphia: Westminster Press, 1972.

Douglas, James Dixon, ed., *The New Bible Dictionary*. Grand Rapids: Eerdmans, 1962.

Dowley, Tim. ed., *Eerdmans' Handbook to the History of Christianity*. Grand Rapids: Eerdmans, 1977.

Edersheim, the Reverend Alfred. *The Life and Times of Jesus the Messiah*. Vols. 1 and 2. New York: Longmans, Green, 1910.

Josephus, Flavius. *Complete Works*. Grand Rapids: Kregel Publications, 1960.

Kroll, Woodrow. *Bible Country: A Journey Through the Holy Land*. Lincoln, NE: Back to the Bible, 1992.

Lindsey, Hal. *A Prophetical Walk Through the Holy Land*. Eugene, OR: Harvest House, 1983.

May, Herbert G., ed., *Oxford Bible Atlas*. 2nd ed. London and New York: Oxford University Press, 1974.

Richards, Lawrence O., ed., *The Revell Bible Dictionary*. Grand Rapids: F. H. Revell, 1990.

Rogness, Alvin R., and Jean Roger. *The Land of Jesus*. Minneapolis: Augsburg Publishers, 1976.

Thompson, J. A. *Handbook of Life in Bible Times*. Downers Grove, IL: InterVarsity Press, 1986.

Walvoord, J. F., and R. B. Zuck. *The Bible Knowledge Commentary: An Exposition of the Scriptures*. Wheaton, IL: Victor Books, 1983.